CHILDREN'S DOVER

Scottish Fairy Tales

DONALD A. MACKENZIE

Illustrated by John Green

DOVER PUBLICATIONS, INC.
Mineola, New York

DOVER CHILDREN'S THRIFT CLASSICS
EDITOR OF THIS VOLUME: TOM CRAWFORD

Copyright

Copyright © 1997 by Dover Publications, Inc.
All rights reserved under Pan American and International Copyright Conventions.

Published in Canada by General Publishing Company, Ltd., 30 Lesmill Road, Don Mills, Toronto, Ontario.
Published in the United Kingdom by Constable and Company, Ltd., 3 The Lanchesters, 162–164 Fulham Palace Road, London W6 9ER.

Bibliographical Note

This Dover edition, first published in 1997, is a new selection of 8 fairy tales from *Wonder Tales from Scottish Myth and Legend,* originally published by Frederick A. Stokes Company, New York, in 1917. The illustrations have been prepared specially for the present edition.

Library of Congress Cataloging-in-Publication Data

Mackenzie, Donald Alexander, 1873–1936.
    [Wonder tales from Scottish myth & legend]
    Scottish fairy tales / Donald A. Mackenzie ; illustrated by John Green.
       p.   cm. — (Dover children's thrift classics)
A new selection of 8 fairy tales from Wonder tales from Scottish myth and legend, originally published by Frederick A. Stokes Company, New York, in 1917.
    Summary: A collection of eight Scottish fairy tales, including "Battle of the Fairy Kings," "Conall and the Thunder Hag," and "Land of Green Mountains."
    ISBN 0-486-29900-7 (pbk.)
    1. Fairy tales—Scotland. [1. Fairy tales. 2. Folklore—Scotland.]
I. Green, John, 1948– ill. II. Title. III. Series.
PZ7.M179Sc 1997
[398.2]—dc21   97-19553
                                                    CIP
                                                    AC

Manufactured in the United States of America
Dover Publications, Inc., 31 East 2nd Street, Mineola, N.Y. 11501

Contents

One fairy king has great fame as an archer;
once a day he shoots an arrow across the valley.

Battle of the Fairy Kings

THERE ARE TWO mountains that overlook the Spey valley, one to the east and one to the west, and a fairy king dwells on each of them. They are both sons of Beira, Queen of Winter. One fairy king is white, and has great fame as an archer; he has a silver bow and arrows of gold, and once a day he shoots an arrow across the valley. The other fairy king is black as the raven, and on his left breast there is a red spot. He has no weapon, but is still terrible in battle, because he can make himself invisible at will. When he does so, nothing remains in sight except the red spot. He has great strength, and when he goes against his enemies he seizes them unawares and throws them to the ground. No matter how well they are armed, his enemies tremble when the invisible fairy comes against them. All they see is a red spot moving about in the air.

Now, the white fairy has a fair bride whose name is Face-of-Light. It is a great joy to her to wander among the mountains where herds of deer crop the green grass, and through the valley where cornfields rustle in soft winds and fragrant flowers bloom fair to see. The black fairy has no bride, and is jealous of the white fairy because his days are filled with joy by the beauty of Face-of-Light. These two fairies have always been enemies. The black fairy keeps out of sight of the famous archer, fearing his arrows of gold.

One summer evening when the twilight shadows were lengthening and deepening across the valley, Face-of-Light tripped merrily over the grassy banks, gathering wild flowers. Silence had fallen on the world; no bird sang and no wind whispered, the lakes were asleep, and the shrunken river made scarcely a sound louder than the sigh of a sleeping babe; it was no longer bright when Face-of-Light turned away from it.

The black fairy looked out from his mountain home. He knew that the white fairy had lain down to rest, and

Suddenly a great black hand was thrust out from a thick clump of bushes.

he watched Face-of-Light gathering wild flowers. Nearer and nearer she came to his dwelling, and he crept into a deep forest which conceals the entrance to his mountain, and waited to seize her. Face-of-Light, never dreaming of her peril, tripped towards the edge of the forest; and, seeing many flowers growing beneath the trees, went in to pluck them. She made the forest bright with her beauty, and the flowers grew fairer as she drew near them. Suddenly a great black hand was thrust out from a thick clump of bushes. The hand seized her, and she shrieked in terror and struggled to escape. The white fairy heard her cries, which pierced the air like the keen long whistle of the curlew, leaped up, and looked forth from his mountain top. In a moment he knew what had happened. Face-of-Light had been seized by his enemy, the black fairy, who was dragging her to a dark dungeon in the middle of his mountain. The white fairy was unable to go to her rescue for two reasons. Like his dark enemy, he could not pass the utmost limits of his mountain house, and having already shot a golden arrow that day, he could not shoot another until a new day had dawned.

Night came on, and the black fairy climbed to the top of his mountain, where he danced with joy because he had taken captive the bride of his enemy. The white fairy was stricken with sorrow, and when he heard the cries of Face-of-Light coming from the dungeon, he fell down in a faint.

All night long Face-of-Light sobbed and wept, while the black fairy danced on the mountain top and sang songs of triumph. He danced so fast that he raised a wind which swept down the valley and shook the trees from sleep, so that they moaned and sighed all night long. The cries of Face-of-Light were heard by human beings, and those who were awakened said one to another: "Listen to the hag of night. How terrible are her cries!"

Not until the dawn began to break did the white fairy recover from his faint. Just when the first shaft of grey light pierced the eastern sky, he opened his eyes. Then he remembered his sorrow and wept softly. His tears fell as dew on the flowers and the grass.

Weeping, he climbed his mountain, and then wandered round about the crest of it. His heart was heavy for the loss of Face-of-Light, and when he listened he heard her moaning in her dark prison. The black fairy had ceased to dance. He stood upright on the highest point of his mountain house, and shouted to his enemy: "Ha! Face-of-Light is my prisoner." Then suddenly he was silent. He saw the white fairy stringing his silver bow and then drawing from his shining quiver a bright golden arrow.

"Ha!" cried the black fairy, "would you dare shoot at me?"

"Set free Face-of-Light, or I shall shoot," the white fairy replied. His face was white as snow and hard as ice.

The black fairy laughed, and willed himself to become invisible, and then, just as the white fairy raised his bow to take aim, his enemy vanished from sight. No part of him could be seen but the great red spot on his left breast, which seemed to float in the air.

For a moment the white fairy, gazing eastward, looked with wonder at the red spot which grew brighter and brighter. His bow was bent, and his golden arrow was held ready for flight.

The sound of defiant laughter came down the wind as the black fairy, now invisible, danced with joy on his mountain top.

To and fro swayed the red spot, and the white fairy thought he would shoot at it. His aim was true and his arm was strong. Straight from the bow flew the bright golden arrow. It darted through the air with lightning speed and struck the red spot, which, be it known, was

The golden arrow darted through the air with lightning speed and struck the heart of the black fairy.

the heart of the black fairy. A shriek rang out across the valley. It was the death shriek of the black fairy, who fell down on the bare rock and died. His life-blood streamed forth, and the whole eastern sky was covered with it. In the midst of the redness gleamed the bright golden arrow of the white fairy.

No sooner was the black fairy slain than Face-of-Light was set free. The doors of her dungeon flew open, and she came forth in all her beauty. When she did so, the mountains and the valley were made bright, the river sparkled in the light, and the lakes flashed like polished silver. All the land was made glad when Face-of-Light was set free from her dark prison. The slumbering flowers opened their eyes to gaze upon her, and the birds broke forth in merry song, while the white fairy smiled and danced with joy.

The black fairy lay dead and invisible on his mountain top until evening came on. Then Beira came to visit him. When she found that her son had been slain, she took from her bag a pot of healing balsam and rubbed it on his wound. Then she rubbed the balsam on his eyes and on his lips. When she did this, he came to life, and began once again to plot evil against the white fairy and his beautiful bride.

The Princess of Land-under-Waves

WHEN NO WIND blows and the surface of the sea is clear as crystal, the beauties of Land-under-Waves are revealed to human eyes. It is a fair country with green valleys through which flow silver streams, and the pebbles in the beds of the streams are flashing gems of varied hues. There are deep forests that glitter in eternal sunshine, and bright flowers that never fade. Rocks are of gold, and the sand is dust of silver.

On a calm morning in May, the Feans, who were great warriors in ancient Scotland, being the offspring of gods and goddesses, were sitting beside the Red Cataract, below which salmon moved slowly, resting themselves before they began to leap towards the higher waters of the stream. The sun was shining bright, and the sea was without a ripple. With eyes of wonder the Feans gazed on the beauties of Land-under-Waves. None spoke, so deeply were they absorbed. They saw the silver sands, the rocks of gold, the gleaming forests, the beautiful flowers, and the bright streams that flow over beds covered with flashing gems.

As they gazed, a boat came over the sea, and there was but one person in it.

Said Oscar: "Who comes this way? Is it the princess of Land-under-Waves?"

A year and a day before, Finn, King of the Feans, and

his men had rescued the princess from the Dark Prince-of-Storm, a powerful warrior who meant to seize her father's kingdom and make her his bride.

Finn looked seaward and said: "No, it is not the princess who comes here, but a young man."

The boat drew swiftly towards the shore, and when the man was within calling distance he hailed Finn with words of greeting and praise.

"Who are you, and where do you come from?" Finn asked.

Said the man: "I am the messenger of the princess of Land-under-Waves. She is ill, and seems ready to die."

There was great sorrow among the Feans when they heard the sad tidings.

"What is your message from the fair princess?" Finn asked.

Said the man: "She bids you to remember your promise to help her in time of need."

"I have never forgotten my promise," Finn told him, "and am ready now to fulfil it."

Said the man: "Then ask Jeermit, the healer, to come with me so that he may give healing to the Princess Under-Waves."

Finn made a sign to Jeermit, and he rose up and went down the beach and entered the boat. Then the boat went out over the sea towards the Far Blue Isle, and it went swiftly until it reached the sea-cave through which one must pass to enter Land-under-Waves.

Now Jeermit was the fairest of all the members of the Fean band. His father was Angus-the-Ever-Young, who conferred upon him the power to give healing for wounds and sickness. Jeermit had knowledge of curative herbs and life-giving waters, and he had the power, by touching a sufferer, to prolong life until he found the means to cure.

Jeermit was taken through the sea-cave of the Far Blue Isle, and for a time he saw nothing, so thick was the darkness; but he heard the splashing of waves against the rocks. At length light broke forth, and the boat grounded. Jeermit stepped out, and found himself

Jeermit was taken through the sea-cave of the Far Blue Isle and heard the splashing of waves against the rocks.

on a broad level plain. The boatman walked in front, and Jeermit followed him. They went on and on, and it seemed that their journey would never end. Jeermit saw a clump of red moss, and plucked some and went on. Before long he saw another clump, and plucked some more. A third time he came to a red moss clump, and from it, too, he plucked a portion. The boatman still led on and on, yet Jeermit never felt weary.

At length Jeermit saw before him a golden castle. He spoke to the boatman, saying: "Whose castle is that?"

Said the boatman: "It is the castle of King Under-Waves, and the princess lies within."

Jeermit entered the castle. He saw many courtiers with pale faces. None spoke: all were hushed to silence with grief. The queen came towards him, and she seized his right hand and led him towards the chamber in which the dying princess lay.

Jeermit knelt beside her, and when he touched her the power of his healing entered her veins, and she opened her eyes. As soon as she beheld Jeermit of the Feans she smiled a sweet smile, and all who were in the chamber smiled, too.

"I feel stronger already," the princess told Jeermit. "Great is the joy I feel to behold you. But the sickness has not yet left me, and I fear I shall die."

"I have three portions of red moss," said Jeermit. "If you will take them in a drink they will heal you, because they are the three life drops of your heart."

"Alas!" the princess exclaimed, "I cannot drink of any water now except from the cup of the King of the Plain-of-Wonder."

Now, great as was Jeermit's knowledge, he had never heard before of this magic cup.

"A wise woman has told that if I take three swallows from this cup I shall be cured," said the princess. "She said also that when I drink I must swallow the three portions of red moss from the Wide-Bare-Plain. The moss of healing you have already found, O Jeermit. But no man shall ever gain possession of the magic cup of the King of the Plain-of-Wonder, and I shall not there-fore get it, and must die."

*Jeermit knelt beside her, and when he touched her
the power of his healing entered her veins.*

Said Jeermit: "There is not in the world above the sea, or the world below the sea, a single man who will keep the cup from me. Tell me where dwells the King of the Plain-of-Wonder. Is his palace far distant from here?"

"No, it is not far distant," the princess told him. "Plain-of-Wonder is the kingdom next to that of my father. The two kingdoms are divided by a river. You may reach that river, O Jeermit, but you may never be able to cross it."

Said Jeermit: "I now lay healing spells upon you, and you shall live until I return with the magic cup."

When he had spoken thus, he rose up and walked out of the castle. The courtiers who had been sad when he entered were merry as he went away, and those who had been silent spoke one to another words of comfort and hope, because Jeermit had laid healing spells upon the princess.

The King and the Queen of Land-under-Waves bade the healer of the Feans farewell, and wished him a safe and speedy journey.

Jeermit went on alone in the direction of the Plain-of-Wonder. He went on and on until he reached the river of which the princess had spoken. Then he walked up and down the river bank searching for a place to cross, but he could not find one.

"I cannot cross over," he said aloud. "The princess has spoken truly."

As he spoke a little brown man rose up out of the river. "Jeermit," he said, "you are now in much trouble."

Said Jeermit: "Indeed I am. You have spoken wisely."

"What would you give to one who would help you in your trouble?"

"Whatever he may ask of me."

"All I ask for," said the brown man, "is your good will."

"That you get freely," said Jeermit to him.

"I shall carry you across the river," said the little man.

"I shall carry you across the river," said the little man.

"You cannot do that."

"Yes, indeed I can."

He stretched forth his hands and took Jeermit on his back, and walked across the river with him, treading the surface as if it were hard ground.

As they crossed the river they passed an island over which hovered a dark mist.

"What island is that?" asked Jeermit.

"Its name," the brown man told him, "is Cold-Isle-of-the-Dead. There is a well on the island, and the water of it is healing water."

They reached the opposite bank, and the brown man said: "You are going to the palace of King Ian of Wonder-Plain."

"I am."

"You desire to obtain the Cup of Healing."

"That is true."

"May you get it," said the brown man, who thereupon entered the river.

Before he disappeared he spoke again and said: "Do you know where you are now?"

"In the Kingdom of Plain-of-Wonder," Jeermit said.

"That is true," said the little brown man. "It is also Land-under-Mountains. This river divides Land-under-Mountains from Land-under-Waves."

Jeermit was about to ask a question, but before he could speak the little brown man vanished from before his eyes.

Jeermit went on and on. There was no sun above him and yet all the land was bright. No darkness ever comes to Land-under-Mountains, and there is no morning there and no evening, but always endless day.

Jeermit went on and on until he saw a silver castle with a roof of gleaming crystal. The doors were shut, and guarded by armed warriors.

Jeermit blew a blast on his horn, and called out, "Open and let me in."

A warrior went towards him with drawn sword. Jeermit flung his spear and killed the warrior.

Then the doors of the castle were opened and King Ian came forth.

"Who are you, and where do you come from?" he asked sternly.

*Jeermit blew a blast on his horn,
and called out, "Open and let me in."*

"I am Jeermit," was the answer he received.

"Son of Angus-the-Ever-Young, you are welcome," exclaimed the king. "Why did you not send a message that you were coming? It is disturbing to think you have slain my greatest warrior."

Said Jeermit: "Give him a drink of the water in the Cup of Healing."

"Bring forth the cup!" the king called.

The cup was brought forth, and the king gave it to Jeermit, saying: "There is no power in the cup unless it .is placed in the hands of either Angus or his son."

Jeermit touched the slain warrior's lips with the cup. He poured drops of the water into the man's mouth, and he sat up. Then he drank all the water in the cup, and rose to his feet strong and well again, for his wound had been healed.

Said Jeermit to the king: "I have come here to obtain this cup, and will now take it with me and go away."

"So be it," answered the king. "I give you the cup freely. But remember that there is no longer any healing in it, for my mighty warrior has drunk the magic water."

Jeermit was not too well pleased when the King of Wonder-Plain said this. "No matter," said he; "I shall take the cup with me."

"I will send a boat to take you across the river and past the Cold-Isle-of-the-Dead," the king said.

Said Jeermit: "I thank you, but I have no need of a boat."

"May you return soon," the king said with a smile, for he believed that Jeermit would never be able to cross the river or pass the Cold-Isle-of-the-Dead.

Jeermit said farewell to the king and went away, as he had come, all alone. He went on and on until he reached the river. Then he sat down, and gloomy thoughts entered his mind. He had obtained the cup, but it was empty; he had returned to the river and could not cross it.

"Alas!" he exclaimed aloud, "my errand is fruitless. The cup is of no use to me, and I cannot cross the river, and must return in shame to the King of Wonder-Plain."

As he spoke the little brown man rose out of the river.

"You are again in great trouble, Jeermit," he said.

"Indeed, I am," answered the son of Angus. "I got what I went for, but it is useless, and I cannot cross the river."

"I shall carry you," said the little brown man.

"So be it," Jeermit answered.

The little brown man walked over the river with Jeermit on his shoulders, and went towards the Cold-Isle-of-the-Dead.

As he spoke the little brown man rose out of the river.

"Where are you carrying me now?" asked Jeermit with fear in his heart.

Said the little brown man: "You desire to heal the daughter of King Under-Waves."

"That is true."

"Your cup is empty, and you must fill it at the Well of Healing, on the Cold-Isle-of-the-Dead. That is why I am carrying you towards the isle. You must not get off my back or set foot on the shore, else you will never be able to leave it. But have no fear. I shall kneel down beside the well, and you can dip the cup in it, and carry off enough water to heal the princess."

Jeermit was well pleased to hear these words, for he knew that the little brown man was indeed his friend. He obtained the healing water in the manner that was promised. Then the little brown man carried him to the opposite bank of the river, and set him down on the border of Land-under-Waves.

"Now you are happy-hearted," said the little brown man.

"Happy-hearted indeed," Jeermit answered.

"Before I bid you farewell I shall give you good advice," said the little brown man.

"Why have you helped me as you have done?" Jeermit asked.

"Because your heart is warm, and you desire to do good to others," said the little brown man. "Men who do good to others will always find friends in the Land of the Living, in the Land of the Dead, in Land-under-Waves, and in Land-under-Mountains."

"I thank you," Jeermit said. "Now I am ready for your good advice, knowing that your friendship is true and lasting."

Said the little brown man: "You may give the princess water from the Cup of Healing, but she will not be cured unless you drop into the water three portions of red moss."

"I have already found these portions on the broad level plain."

"That is well," said the other. "Now I have more advice to offer you. When the princess is healed the king

"I will follow your advice," Jeermit promised.

will offer you choice of reward. Take no thing he offers, but ask for a boat to carry you home again."

"I will follow your advice," Jeermit promised.

Then the two parted, and Jeermit went on and on until he came to the golden palace of King Under-Waves. The princess welcomed him when he was brought into her room, and said, "No man ever before was given the cup you now carry."

Said Jeermit: "For your sake I should have got it, even if I had to fight an army."

"I feared greatly that you would never return," sighed the princess.

Jeermit put into the Cup of Healing the three portions of blood-red moss which he had found, and told the princess to drink.

Three times she drank, and each time she swallowed a portion of red moss. When she drank the last drop, having swallowed the third portion of red moss, she said: "Now I am healed. Let a feast be made ready, and I shall sit at the table with you."

There was great joy and merriment in the castle when the feast was held. Sorrow was forgotten and music was played. When the feast was over, the king spoke to Jeermit and said: "I would like to reward you for healing my daughter, the princess. I shall give you as much silver and gold as you desire, and you shall marry my daughter and become the heir to my throne."

Said Jeermit: "If I marry your daughter I cannot again return to my own land."

"No, you cannot again return, except on rare and short visits. But here you will spend happy days, and everyone shall honour you."

Said Jeermit: "The only reward I ask for, O king, is a small one indeed."

"I promise to give you whatever you ask for."

Said Jeermit: "Give me a boat, so that I may return again to my own land, which is very dear to me, and to my friends and kinsmen, the Feans, whom I love, and to Finn mac Cool, the great chief of men."

"Your wish is granted," the king said.

Three times she drank,
and each time she swallowed a portion of red moss.

Then Jeermit said farewell to all who were in the castle, and when he parted with the princess she said: "I shall never forget you, Jeermit. You found me in suffering and gave me relief; you found me dying and gave me back my life again. When you return to your own land remember me, for I shall never pass an hour of life without thinking of you with joy and thankfulness."

Jeermit crossed the level plain once again, and reached the place where the boat in which he had come lay safely moored. The boatman went into it and seized the oars, and Jeermit went in after him. Then the boat sped through the deep dark tunnel, where the waves splash unseen against the rocks, and passed out of the cave on the shore of the Far Blue Isle. The boat then went speedily over the sea, and while it was still far off, Finn saw it coming. All the Feans gathered on the shore to bid Jeermit welcome.

"Long have we waited for you, son of Angus," Finn said.

"What time has passed since I went away?" asked Jeermit, for it seemed to him that he had been absent for no more than a day and a night.

"Seven long years have passed since we said farewell," Finn told him, "and we feared greatly that you would never again come back to us."

Said Jeermit: "In the lands I visited there is no night, and no change in the year. Glad am I to return home once again."

Then they all went to Finn's house, and a great feast was held in honour of Jeermit, who brought back with him the Cup of Healing which he had received from the King of Wonder-Plain.

Conall and the Thunder Hag

AMONG THE WITCHES who served Beira, Queen of Winter, was the Thunder Hag. When Angus, King of Summer, began to reign she fled across the ocean to a lonely island, where she plotted to get even by bringing disaster to man and beast, because they had rejoiced when Beira was overcome by Angus.

One day in midsummer, when all the land was bathed in warm, bright sunshine and the sea was lulled to sleep, the Thunder Hag came over Scotland in a black chariot drawn by fierce red hounds and surrounded by heavy clouds. The sky was darkened, and as the hag drew near, the rattling of the chariot wheels and the baying of the hounds sounded loud and frightful. She rode from sea to sea, over hill and moor, and threw fireballs at the deep forests, which set them ablaze. Terror spread through the land as the chariot passed in smoke and clouds.

On the next day the hag came back. She threw more fireballs on forests of fir and silver birch, and they burned fiercely. Dry heather on the moors and the sun-dried grass were also swept by flame.

The king was greatly troubled, and he sent forth his chief warriors to slay the hag; but they fled in terror when they saw her coming near.

On the third day she returned. Then the king called for Conall Curlew, the fearless hero, and spoke to him, saying: "My kingdom will be destroyed if the hag is not slain. I need your help, O brave and noble one."

Said Conall: "I shall fight against the hag, O king, and if I do not slay her today, I may slay her tomorrow."

Conall went forth, and when he saw and heard the chariot drawing near he went up to the summit of a

Conall waited to attack the hag,
but she kept herself hidden behind a cloud.

high mountain and waited to attack her. But the hag kept herself hidden behind a cloud which surrounded the chariot. Conall had to return to the king without having done anything.

"I could not see the hag because of the dark cloud," he said.

"If she comes again tomorrow," the king said, "you may fare better."

Conall then made preparations for the next coming of the hag. He went out into the fields that were near the royal castle, and separated all the lambs from the sheep, all the calves from the cows, and all the foals from the mares. When morning came there was great commotion among the animals.

There never was heard before such a bleating of sheep, such a lowing of cattle, or neighing of mares, and it was piteous to hear the cries of the lambs, and the calves, and the foals which were taken from their mothers. The men were filled with wonder at the thing Conall had done, nor could they understand why he had done it, and the hearts of the women were touched by the cries of the young animals, and they wept to hear them.

It was indeed a morning of sorrow and wailing when the cloud in which the hag's chariot was hidden came near the castle. The cloud darkened the heavens, and when it passed over the wooded hill the fireballs set the trees in flame, and all the people fled before the cloud and concealed themselves in caves and in holes in the ground—all except the warriors, who waited, trembling, with deep eyes and pale faces.

Conall stood alone on a green hill, and his spear was in his hand.

When the cloud came over the valley of the castle, the hag heard the cries of the animals ringing in her ears, and so great was her curiosity that she peered over the edge of the black cloud.

Great fear fell on the hearts of the warriors when they saw the horrible face of the grey-headed hag; but Conall was a man without fear, and he was waiting for the hag to reveal herself.

*As soon as he saw her, he swung his right arm over his shoulder,
and he cast the spear towards the cloud.*

As soon as he saw her, he swung his right arm over his shoulder, and he cast the spear towards the cloud. The swallow does not dart swifter than the spear of Conall darted through the air.

The hag was wounded, and threw wide her horrible paws and sank down within the chariot. She called to the black hounds: "Race quickly!" and they ran swiftly towards the west. The sound of the rattling of the chariot wheels grew fainter and fainter as it passed out of sight.

The clouds which the hag passed over swiftly in her flight were torn apart, and rain fell in torrents, quenching the fires that were in the woods and on the moors.

There was great rejoicing in the land because of the mighty deed done by Conall, and the king honoured that noble hero by placing a gold ring on his finger, a gold armband on his arm, and a gold necklace on his neck.

There was peace and prosperity in the land after that. The hag did not return again, so greatly did she dread Conall Curlew, the hero of heroes.

The Story of Finlay and the Giants

FINLAY THE HUNTER lived with his sister in a lonely little house among the mountains, and near at hand there were giants who were descendants of Beira, the Queen of Winter. This giant clan was ruled over by a witch who was very old and fierce and cunning. She had heaps of silver and gold in her cave, and also a gold-hilted magic sword and a magic wand. When she struck a stone pillar with this wand it became a warrior, and if she put the gold-hilted sword into his hand, the greatest and strongest hero in the world would be unable to combat against him with success.

Every day that Finlay went out to hunt he warned his sister, saying: "Do not open the windows on the north side of the house, or let the fire go out."

His sister did not, however, always listen to his warning. One day she shut the windows on the south side of the house, and opened those on the north side, and allowed the fire to go out.

She wondered what would happen, and she had not long to wait, for a young giant came towards the house and entered it. He had assumed a handsome form, and spoke pleasantly to Finlay's sister. They became very friendly, and the giant made the foolish girl promise not to tell her brother of his visits. After that the girl began to quarrel with Finlay. This went on for a time.

One day when Finlay was returning to his home he

saw a little hut in a place where no hut used to be. He wondered who dwelt in it, and walked towards the door and entered. He saw an old woman sitting on the floor, and she welcomed him.

"Sit down," she said. "Your name is Finlay."

"That is true," answered he; "who are you and where are you from?"

"I am called Wise Woman," she answered. "I have come here to protect and guide you. Alas! you do not know that you are in danger of your life. A young giant has bewitched your sister, and is waiting to kill you this very day with a sharp blue sword."

"Alas!" cried Finlay, who sorrowed to think of his sister.

Having been warned, the hunter was prepared. When he returned home he set his fierce dogs on the giant,

After seeing the fierce dogs, the giant fled shrieking towards his cave.

and threw a pot of boiling water over him. The giant fled shrieking towards his cave, and Finlay's sister followed him.

Then the hunter was left alone in the house. His heart shook with terror because he feared that one of the older giants would come to avenge the injury done to the young giant.

He had good reason to be afraid. As soon as the young giant reached the cave, his brother cried: "I shall go forth and deal with the hunter."

"I had better go myself," his father said fiercely.

"It is I who should go," growled the fierce grey witch.

"I spoke first," urged the young giant's brother, and sprang towards the mouth of the cave in the gathering dusk.

Finlay waited alone in his little house. The door was shut and securely barred, and the peat fire glowed bright and warm, yet he shivered with the coldness of terror. He listened long and anxiously, and at length heard a growing noise like distant thunder. Stones rumbled down the hillside as the giant raced on, and when he entered a bog the mud splashed heavily against the cliffs. Finlay knew then that a giant was coming, and before long he heard his voice roaring outside the door: "Fith! Foth! Foogie! The door is shut against a stranger. Open and let me in." He did not wait for Finlay to answer, but burst the door open with a blow. The hunter stood behind the fire which burned in the middle of the room, his bow in his hand and an arrow ready. He fired as the giant entered, but did not kill him. The giant shrieked and leaped towards Finlay, but the dogs attacked him fiercely. Then the hunter shot another arrow from his bow and killed the giant.

Next morning Finlay hurried to the hut of Wise Woman, taking with him the giant's head.

"Well, brave lad," she exclaimed, "how did you do last night?"

Finlay told her all that had taken place, and explained that it was owing to the help given him by the dogs he was able to kill the giant.

"There is need of the dogs," Wise Woman said, "but the day of their great need has yet to come."

That evening Finlay again sat alone in his house, wondering what would happen next. No sooner did night come on than he heard a noise like distant thunder, but much louder than on the night before. Great boulders rumbled down the hillside, and mud splashed on the cliffs. Another and more terrible giant was coming, seeking to be avenged.

"Thoth! Thoth! Foogie!" roared his terrible voice outside the house. "I smell a man inside. Open the door that I may enter. Although you killed my son last night, you shall not kill me."

He burst the door open, and as he did so the house shook. Finlay feared the roof was about to fall upon him, but he feared more when he saw the giant in the firelight, for the monster had five heads.

He drew his bow and shot an arrow. The giant paused. Finlay shot a second arrow, which, like the first, wounded the monster, but did not kill him. Then the hunter drew his sword and struck him hard, but his wounds were not fatal. The giant stretched out his horrible hands to seize Finlay, but the dogs leaped at him, and a fierce struggle took place, but in the end Finlay triumphed, and the giant was killed.

Next morning the hunter went to the hut of Wise Woman, and told her of the night of terror and the long and deadly combat. "The dogs," he said, "helped me. Except for the dogs I would have been defeated."

Said Wise Woman: "There is need for the dogs, but

the day of their greatest need has yet to come. Tonight the fierce grey witch will try to avenge the death of her husband and son. Beware of her, O brave lad! She will not come raging and roaring like the giants, but gently and quietly. She will call to you in a soft and mild voice, asking you to let her in. But, remember, she wants to take your life. Do as I instruct you and all will be well."

Wise Woman then gave him instructions, and he went home. When night came on there was silence all around. Finlay waited alone, listening intently, and the silence terrified him more than the noises like distant thunder he had heard on the two previous nights. He shook and shivered beside the warm bright peat fire, waiting and waiting and listening. At length he sprang up suddenly, for he heard a rustling sound like the wind stirring dead leaves. A moment later a weak, patient voice outside the door called: "I am old and weary. I have need of food and of shelter for the night. Open and let me in."

Finlay went to the door and answered: "I shall let you in, old woman, if you promise to be civil and polite, and not hurt me."

Said the witch: "Oh! I shall be no trouble. I promise to be civil and polite. Let me enter your house."

Finlay opened the door, and the witch walked in. She looked like a poor, frail old woman, and seemed to be very weary. When she had curtsied to Finlay, she sat down on one side of the fire. Finlay sat down on the opposite side.

The witch stretched out her hands to warm them, and began to look about her. Finlay's three dogs were prowling up and down the room, snarling angrily and showing their teeth.

"These are fierce dogs," the widow said. "Arise and tie them with rope."

"The dogs will not do any harm to a peaceful old woman," said Finlay.

"Tie them up in any case, I pray you. I dislike angry dogs."

"I cannot do that, old woman, because I have nothing to tie them with."

Said the witch: "I will give you three red ribbons from my cap. They are strong enough to hold a big ship at anchor."

Finlay took the red ribbons from her and pretended to tie up the dogs. But he only made them lie down in a corner.

"Have you tied up the dogs?" asked the witch very softly.

Finlay took the red ribbons from her and pretended to tie up the dogs.

"You can see for yourself that they are lying now with their necks close together," Finlay answered. The witch looked at the dogs, and believing they had been secured with her magic ribbons, smiled to herself.

She sat beside the fire in silence for a time, and Finlay sat opposite her. After a time the hunter noticed that she was growing bigger and bigger.

"What does this mean?" cried Finlay. "You seem to be growing bigger and bigger."

"Oh, no, my darling!" she answered. "The cold of the night made me shrink, and now I am feeling more comfortable beside your warm bright fire."

There was silence again, and Finlay watched her for a time and then cried: "You are growing bigger, without doubt. You may be pleased or displeased because I say so, but you cannot deny it."

The witch frowned and answered angrily: "I am growing bigger, as you say. What of it? You fear me now, and you have good reason to. You killed my husband last night, and you killed my son on the night before. I shall certainly kill you tonight."

When she had said this she sprang to her feet in full height, and the house shook about her and above. Finlay sprang to his feet also, and as he did so the witch seized him by the hair of his head. Having promised not to injure him inside the house—a promise she could not break—she dragged him outside. The three dogs rose, and sprang through the door after her.

Finlay wrestled fiercely with the witch, and the two twisted and turned back and forth. The mother of the young giant would have killed him without delay, but the dogs kept attacking her, and gave her much trouble. At length, with the help of the dogs, Finlay managed to throw her down. She lay upon one of her arms, and the dogs held the other.

*"I am growing bigger, and you fear me now.
I shall certainly kill you tonight," the witch said angrily.*

"Oh! let me rise to my feet," cried the witch, who had no power to struggle when she lay on the ground.

Said Finlay: "I shall not allow you to rise up."

"Allow me to ransom myself," the witch pleaded.

Said Finlay: "What ransom will you give?"

"I have a trunk of gold and a trunk of silver in my cave. You shall get both," she answered.

Said Finlay: "Having defeated you, these are mine already."

"I will give you a gold-hilted sword which is in my cave," the witch then promised. "He who wields this magic sword will conquer any man or any beast in the world."

Said Finlay: "The sword is mine already."

"I will give you a magic rod if you spare me," the witch cried then. "It is a matchless weapon. It can also work wonders. If you strike a stone pillar with it, the pillar will turn into a warrior, and if you will put the gold-hilted sword in this warrior's hand, he will conquer the world for you."

Said Finlay: "Your wand is mine already by right of conquest. What else have you to offer for ransom?"

"Alas!" the witch cried, "I have nothing else to give you."

Said Finlay: "Then you shall die. The world will be well rid of you."

He killed the fierce witch, and then arose quickly and put red moss on his wounds and sores, so that they might be healed speedily. Next morning he arose and went and informed Wise Woman of what had taken place, saying: "It was chiefly owing to the dogs that the witch was defeated."

Said Wise Woman: "O brave hero! the dogs have now had their day."

Then Finlay told about the treasure in the cave, and

said: "I don't know how I can obtain the gold and silver, the gold-hilted sword, and the magic wand."

Said Wise Woman: "Tonight my daughter and I will go with you to the giants' cave. I will take my own magic wand with me."

When darkness came on, the three went to the cave. They set to work and gathered armfuls of dry heather, which they heaped up at the cave mouth and set on

Finlay drew his bow and said: "I will shoot."

fire, so that the young giant within would be choked by the fumes and scorched by the flames. Soon the giant crawled to the mouth of the cave, panting heavily. He came through the smoke dazed and half blinded. Suddenly a warning light appeared on his forehead.

Finlay drew his bow and said: "I will shoot."

"Do not shoot," Wise Woman warned him. "A wound would only make him fiercer, and the dogs would be of

Finlay struck a stone pillar with the magic wand,
and it became a noble warrior.

no use to you among the fire. If he is allowed to escape out of the glare, the dogs would not see him in the darkness. I shall strike him with my magic wand. I can strike once only, and if I fail he will strike the next blow with the gold-hilted sword which is in his hand."

The giant scattered the fire to get out of the cave, but before he could rise Wise Woman struck him on the head with her magic wand, and he fell down dead.

When they entered the cave they found that Finlay's sister was within. But she was dead; she had perished in her cave prison.

Finlay took out all the treasure that was in the cave, and carried it to the hut of Wise Woman. Then he tested the magic wand. He struck a stone pillar with it, and the pillar became a warrior. Then he struck the warrior, and he became a stone pillar again.

"This is wonderful," Finlay exclaimed.

"It is indeed," said Wise Woman. Then she told him that he must visit the king next day and inform him of all that had taken place, and she made him take a vow not to enter the palace.

Next day Finlay set out to the palace of the king. When he reached it he told the royal servants to inform the king that the great giants had been killed.

Said the king: "Let the brave hero come inside."

Finlay, however, declined to enter the palace, and sent him word, saying: "I dare not enter your palace, as I have a vow to fulfil."

The king came outside and spoke to Finlay, saying: "Come within. I shall give you my daughter, the princess, in marriage. You shall also have half of my kingdom as long as I live, and the rest shall be yours when I die."

Said Finlay: "I give you thanks, O king, but I cannot enter."

When he had said this, he walked towards a grey stone pillar and struck it with the magic wand. The pillar became a noble warrior. Then he struck the warrior, and he became a pillar again. The king was greatly astonished, and exclaimed: "I have never seen anything like this before."

He went into the palace to give orders about Finlay, whom he wished to detain, but when he came out again he found that the hunter had gone.

The king sent out foot-runners and horsemen to search throughout the kingdom for Finlay, but they returned without having caught sight of him.

Finlay married the daughter of Wise Woman, and he prospered.

The Story of Michael Scott

MICHAEL SCOTT, who lived during the thirteenth century, was known far and near as a great scholar, and it is told that he had dealings with the fairies and other spirits. When he wanted to erect a house or a bridge, he called the "wee folk" to his aid, and they did the work for him in a single night. He had great skill as a healer of wounds and curer of diseases, and the people called him a magician.

When Michael was a young man he set out on a journey to Edinburgh with two companions. They travelled on foot, and one day, when they were climbing a high hill, they sat down to rest. No sooner had they done so than they heard a loud hissing sound. They looked in the direction of the sound, and saw with horror a great white serpent, curved in wheel shape, rolling towards them at a rapid speed. It was evident that the monster was going to attack them, and when it began to roll up the hillside as swiftly as it had crossed the moor, Michael's two companions sprang to their feet and ran away, shouting with terror. Michael was a man who knew no fear, and he made up his mind to attack the serpent. He stood waiting for it, with his walking stick firmly grasped in his right hand.

When the serpent came close to Michael it uncurved its body and, throwing itself into a coil, raised its head to strike, its jaws gaping wide and its forked tongue thrust out like an arrow. Michael at once raised his stick, and struck the monster so fierce a blow that he cut its body into three parts. Then he turned away, and called upon his friends to wait for him. They heard his voice, stopped running, and gazed upon him with wonder as he walked towards them very calmly and at an easy pace. It was a great relief to them to learn from Michael that he had slain the frightening monster.

They walked on together, and had not gone far when they came to a house in which lived a wise old woman. As the sun was beginning to set and it would soon be dark, they asked her for a night's lodging, and she invited them to enter the house. One of the men then told her of their adventure with the rolling serpent which Michael had slain.

Said the Wise Woman: "Are you sure the white serpent is dead?"

"It must be dead," Michael answered, "because I cut its body into three parts."

Said the Wise Woman: "This white serpent is no ordinary serpent. It has power to unite the severed parts of its body again. Once before it was attacked by a brave man, who cut it in two. The head part of its body, however, crawled to a stream. After bathing in the stream it crawled back and joined itself to the tail part. The serpent then became whole again, and once more it bathed in the healing waters of the stream. All serpents do this after attacking a human being. If a man has been stung by a serpent, he should hasten to the stream before the serpent can reach it and he will be cured and the serpent will die."

"You have great knowledge of the mysteries," Michael exclaimed with wonder.

Said the Wise Woman: "You have overcome the white serpent this time, but you may not be so fortunate the next time it attacks you. Be assured of this: the serpent will, after it has been healed, lie in wait for you to get revenge. The next time it attacks, you will receive no warning that it is near."

"I shall never cross the high mountain again," Michael declared.

Said the Wise Woman: "The serpent will search for you and find you, no matter where you may be."

"Alas!" Michael exclaimed, "evil is my fate. What can I do to protect myself against the serpent?"

Said the Wise Woman: "Go now to the place where you struck the serpent, and carry away the middle part of its body. Hurry, before it's too late."

Michael took her advice, and asked his companions to go with him; but they were afraid to do so, and he set out alone.

He walked quickly, and soon came to the place where he had struck down the monster. He found the middle part and the tail part of the white serpent's body, but the head part was nowhere to be seen. He knew then that the woman had spoken truly, and, as darkness was coming on, he did not care to search for the stream to which the head part had gone. Lifting up the middle part of the body, which still quivered, he hurried back towards the house of the Wise Woman. The sky darkened, and the stars began to appear. Michael grew uneasy. He felt sure that something was following him at a distance, so he quickened his steps and never looked back. At length he reached the house in safety, and he was glad to find that there were charms above the door which prevented any evil spirit from entering.

The Wise Woman welcomed Michael, and asked him to give her the part of the serpent's body which he had brought with him. He did so willingly, and she thanked him, and said: "Now I shall prepare a meal for you and your companions."

The woman at once set to work and cooked an excellent meal. Michael began to wonder why she showed him and his friends so much kindness and why she was in such high spirits. She laughed and talked as merrily

Lifting up the middle part of the serpent's body, he hurried back to the house of the Wise Woman.

as a girl, and he suspected she had been made happy because he had brought her the middle part of the white serpent's body. He resolved to watch her and find out, if possible, what she was going to do with it.

After eating his supper Michael pretended that he suffered from pain, and went into the kitchen to sit beside the fire. He told the woman that the heat took away the pain, and asked her to allow him to sleep in a chair in front of the fire. She said, "Very well," so he sat down, while his weary companions went to bed. The woman put a pot on the fire, and placed in it the middle part of the serpent's body.

Michael noticed this, but said nothing. He pretended to sleep. The part of the serpent began to sizzle in the pot, and the woman came from another room, lifted off the lid, and looked in. Then she touched the cut of the serpent with her right finger. When she did so a cock crowed on the roof of the house. Michael was startled. He opened his eyes and looked round.

Said the Wise Woman: "I thought you were fast asleep."

"I cannot sleep because of the pain I suffer," Michael told her.

Said the Wise Woman: "If you cannot sleep, you may be of service to me. I am very weary and wish to sleep. I am cooking the part of the serpent. Watch the pot for me, and see that the part does not burn. Call me when it is properly cooked, but be sure not to touch it before you do so."

"I shall not sleep," Michael said, "so I may as well have something to do."

The Wise Woman smiled, and said: "After you call me, I shall cure your trouble." Then she went to her bed and lay down to sleep.

Michael sat watching the pot, and when he found that the portion of the serpent's body was fully cooked, he lifted the pot off the fire. Before calling the old woman, he thought he would first do what she had done when she lifted the lid off the pot. He dipped his finger into the juice of the serpent's body. The tip of his right finger was badly burned, so he thrust it into his mouth. The cock on the roof flapped its wings at once,

*Michael lifted the lid off the pot and dipped his finger
into the juice of the serpent's body.*

and crowed so loudly that the old woman woke up in bed and screamed.

Michael felt that there must be magic in the juice of the serpent. New light and knowledge broke in upon him, and he discovered that he had the power to predict the future, to work magic cures, and to read the minds of other people.

The old woman came out of her room. "You did not call me," she said in a sad voice.

Michael knew what she meant. Had he called her, she would have been the first to taste the juice of the white serpent and receive from it the great power he now himself possessed.

"I killed the serpent," he said, "and had the first right to taste of its juice."

Said the Wise Woman: "I dare not scold you now. Nor need I tell you what powers you possess, for you have become wiser than I am. You can cure diseases, you can foretell and foresee what is to take place, you have power to make the fairies obey your commands, and you can obtain greater knowledge about the hidden mysteries than any other man alive. All that I ask of you is your friendship."

"I give you my friendship willingly," Michael said to her. Then the Wise Woman sat down beside him and asked him many questions about hidden things, and Michael found himself able to answer each one. They sat together talking until dawn. Then Michael awoke his companions, and the woman cooked a breakfast. When Michael bade her good-bye, she said: "Do not forget me, for you owe much to me."

"I shall never forget you," he promised her.

Michael and his companions resumed their journey. They walked until sunset, but did not reach a house.

"Tonight," one of the men said, "we must sleep in the fields."

Michael smiled. "Tonight," said he, "we shall sleep in Edinburgh."

"It is still a day's journey from here," the man reminded him.

Michael laid his stick on the ground and said: "Let us three sit on this stick and see what happens."

His companions laughed, and sat down as he asked them to do. They thought it a great joke.

"Hold tight!" Michael advised them. The men, still amused, grasped the stick in their hands and held it tightly.

*"Let us three sit on this stick
and it will carry us to Edinburgh," Michael said.*

"Stick of mine!" Michael cried, "carry us to Edinburgh."

No sooner did he speak than the stick rose high in the air. The men were terror-stricken as the stick flew towards the clouds and then went forward with the speed of lightning. They shivered with fear and with cold. Snow-flakes fell on them as the stick flew across the sky, for they were higher up than the peak of Ben Nevis. When night was falling and the stars came out one by one, the stick began to descend. Happy were Michael's companions when they came down safely on the outskirts of Edinburgh.

They walked into the town in silence, and the first man they met stood and gazed with wonder upon them in the lamplight.

"Why do you stare at strangers?" Michael asked.

Said the man: "There is snow on your caps and your shoulders."

Having said this, a sudden fear overcame him, and he turned and fled, believing that the three strangers were either wizards or fairies.

Michael shook the snow off his cap and shoulders, and his companions did the same. They then looked for a place to stay, and having eaten their suppers, went to bed.

Next morning Michael found that his companions had risen early and gone away. He knew that they were afraid of him, so he smiled and said to himself: "I bear them no ill will. I prefer now to be alone."

Michael soon became famous as a builder. When he was asked to build a house, he called on the fairies, who were happy to use their enormous powers to help him whenever they could.

In the Kingdom of Seals

THE SEA FAIRIES have grey skin-coverings and re-semble seals. They dwell in cave houses on the borders of Land-under-Waves, where they have a kingdom of their own. They love music and dance, like the green land fairies, and when a harpist or bagpiper plays on the beach they come up to listen, their dark black eyes sparkling with joy. On moonlit nights they hear the mermaids singing on the rocks when human beings are fast asleep, and they call to them: "Sing again the old sea songs; sing again!" All night long the sea fairies call out when mermaids cease to sing, and the mermaids sing again and again to them. When the wind whistles loud and free, and the sea leaps and whirls and swings and cries aloud with wintry merriment, the sea fairies dance with the dancing waves, tossing white petals of foam over their heads, and twining pearls of spray about their necks. They love to hunt the silver salmon in the forests of seaweed and in ocean's deep blue valleys, and far up dark ravines through which flow rivers of sweet mountain waters sparkling with stars.

The sea fairies have a language of their own, and they are also skilled in human speech. When they come ashore they can take the forms of men or women, and turn waves into dark horses with grey manes and long grey tails, and on these they ride over mountain and moor.

There was once a fisherman who visited the palace of the queen of sea fairies, and told on his return all he had seen and all he had heard. He dwelt in a little township near John-o'-Groat's House, and was accustomed to catch fish and seals. When he found that he could earn much money by hunting seals, whose skins make warm winter clothing, he forgot about catching salmon or cod, and worked constantly as a seal-hunter. He crept among the rocks searching for his prey, and visited lonely seal-haunted islands across the Pentland Firth, where he often found the strange sea-prowlers lying on smooth flat ledges of rock fast asleep in the warm sunshine.

In his house he had great bundles of dried sealskins, and people came from a distance to purchase them from him. His fame as a seal-hunter spread far and wide.

One evening a dark stranger rode up to his house, mounted on a black, spirited mare with grey mane and grey tail. He called to the fisherman who came out, and then said: "Make haste and ride with me towards the east. My master desires to do business with you."

"I have no horse," the fisherman answered, "but I shall walk to your master's house tomorrow."

Said the stranger: "Come now. Ride with me. My good mare is fleet-footed and strong."

"As you wish," answered the fisherman, who at once mounted the mare behind the stranger.

The mare turned round and galloped eastward faster than the wind of March. Beach gravel rose in front of her like rock-strewn sea-spray, and a sand-cloud gathered and swept out behind like mountain mists that are scattered before a gale. The fisherman gasped for breath, for although the wind was blowing against his back when he mounted the mare, it blew fiercely in his

The mare galloped fast until she drew near the edge of a precipice.

face as he rode on. The mare went fast and far until she drew near a precipice. At the edge of it she halted suddenly. The fisherman found then that the wind was still blowing seaward, although he had thought it had veered round as he rode. Never before had he sat on the back of so fleet-footed a mare.

Said the stranger: "We have almost reached my master's dwelling."

The fisherman looked round about him with surprise, and saw neither house nor the smoke from the chimney of one. "Where is your master?" he asked.

Said the stranger: "You shall see him presently. Come with me."

As he spoke he walked towards the edge of the precipice and looked over. The fisherman did the same, and saw nothing but the grey lonely sea heaving in a long slow swell, and sea-birds swooping and sliding down the wind.

"Where is your master?" he asked once again.

With that the stranger suddenly clasped the seal-hunter in his arms, and crying, "Come with me," leaped over the edge of the precipice. The mare leaped with her master.

Down, down they fell through the air, scattering the startled sea-birds. Screaming and fluttering, the birds rose in clouds about and above them, and down, ever down, the men and the mare continued to fall till they plunged into the sea, and sank and sank, while the light around them faded into darkness deeper than night. The fisherman wondered to find himself still alive as he passed through the sea depths, seeing nothing, hearing nothing, and still moving swiftly. At length he ceased to sink, and went forward. He suffered no pain or discomfort, nor was he afraid. His only feeling was of wonder, and in the thick, cool darkness he wondered greatly what would happen next. At length he saw a faint green light, and as he went onward the light grew brighter and brighter, until the valleys and peaks and forests of the sea kingdom arose before his eyes. Then he discovered that he was swimming beside the stranger and that they had both been changed into seals.

Said the stranger: "Yonder is my master's house."

The fisherman looked, and saw a township of foam-white houses on the edge of a great sea-forest and fronted by a bank of sea-moss which was green as grass but more beautiful, and very bright. There were crowds of seal-folk in the township. He saw them moving about to and fro, and heard their voices, but he could not understand their speech. Mothers nursed their babes, and young children played games on banks of green sea-moss, and from the brown and golden sea-forest came sounds of music and the shouts of dancers.

Said the stranger: "Here is my master's house. Let us enter."

He led the fisherman towards the door of a great foam-white palace with many bright windows. It was thatched with red seaweed, and the door was of green stone. The door opened as smoothly as a summer wave that moves across a river mouth, and the fisherman entered with his guide. He found himself in a dimly-lighted room, and saw an old grey seal stretched on a bed, and heard him moaning with pain. Beside the bed lay a blood-stained knife, and the fisherman knew at a glance that it was his own. Then he remembered that, not many hours before, he had stabbed a seal, and that it had escaped by plunging into the sea, carrying the knife in its back.

The fisherman was startled to realize that the old seal on the bed was the very one he had tried to kill, and his heart was filled with fear. He threw himself down and begged for forgiveness and mercy, for he feared that he would be put to death.

The guide lifted up the knife and asked: "Have you ever seen this knife before?" He spoke in human language.

"That is my knife, alas!" exclaimed the fisherman.

The fisherman laid his hand on the wound,
and the pain that the seal suffered passed into his hand.

Said the guide: "The wounded seal is my father. Our doctors are unable to cure him. They can do nothing without your help. That is why I visited your house and urged you to come with me. I ask your pardon for deceiving you, O man! but as I love my father greatly, I had to do what I have done."

"Do not ask my pardon," the fisherman said; "I must ask yours. I am sorry and ashamed for having stabbed your father."

Said the guide: "Lay your hand on the wound and wish it to be healed."

The fisherman laid his hand on the wound, and the pain that the seal suffered passed into his hand, but did not remain long. As if by magic, the wound was healed at once. Then the old grey seal rose up strong and well again.

Said the guide: "You have served us well this day, O man!"

When the fisherman had entered the house, all the seals within were weeping tears of sorrow, but they ceased to weep as soon as he had laid his hand on the wound, and when the old seal rose up they all became merry and bright.

The fisherman wondered what would happen next. For a time the seals seemed to forget his presence, but at length his guide spoke to him and said: "Now, O man! you can return to your own home where your wife and children await you. I shall lead you through the sea depths, and take you on my mare across the plain which we crossed when coming here."

"I give you thanks," the fisherman exclaimed.

Said the guide: "Before you leave there is one thing you must do; you must take a vow never again to hunt seals."

The fisherman answered: "Surely, I promise never again to hunt for seals."

Said the guide: "If ever you break your promise you shall die. I advise you to keep it, and as long as you do so you will prosper. Every time you set lines, or cast a net, you will catch much fish. Our seal-servants will help you, and if you wish to reward them for their services, take with you in your boat a harp or bagpipe and play sweet music, for music is the delight of all seals."

The fisherman vowed he would never break his promise, and the guide then led him back to dry land. As soon as he reached the shore he ceased to be a seal and became a man once again. The guide, who had also changed shape, breathed over a great wave and, immediately, it became a dark mare with grey mane and grey tail. He then mounted the mare, and told the fisherman to mount behind him. The mare rose in the air as lightly as wind-tossed spray, and passing through the clouds of startled sea-birds reached the top of the precipice. On she raced at once, raising the gravel in front and a cloud of sand behind. The night was falling and the stars began to appear, but it was not quite dark when the fisherman's house was reached.

The fisherman dismounted, and his guide spoke and said: "Take this from me, and may you live happily."

He handed the fisherman a small bag, and crying: "Farewell! Remember your vow," he turned his mare right round and passed swiftly out of sight.

The fisherman entered his house, and found his wife still there. "You have returned," she said. "How did you fare?"

"I know not yet," he answered. Then he sat down and opened the bag, and to his surprise and delight found it was full of pearls.

*He sat down and opened the bag, and to his surprise
and delight found it was full of pearls.*

His wife uttered a cry of wonder, and said: "From whom did you receive this treasure?"

The fisherman then told all that had taken place, and his wife was amazed to hear him.

"Never again will I hunt seals," he exclaimed. And he kept his word and prospered, and lived happily until the day of his death.

The Maid-of-the-Wave

THE MERMAID, OR, as she is called in Gaelic, Maid-of-the-Wave, has great beauty and is sweet-voiced. Half her body is of fish shape, and glitters like a salmon in sunshine, and she has long copper-colored hair which she loves to comb as she sits on a rock on a lonely shore, gazing in a mirror of silver, and singing a song in praise of her own great beauty. Sometimes, on moonlit nights, she takes off her skin covering and puts on sea-blue garments, and then she seems fairer than any lady in the land.

Once a young farmer was wandering below the cliffs on a beautiful summer night when the wind was still and the silver moon shone through the clear depths of ocean, casting a flood of light through Land-under-Waves. He heard sounds of song and laughter. He crept softly towards a shadowy rock, and, climbing it, looked down on a bank of white sand. There he beheld a company of mermaids dancing in a ring round a maid who was fairest of the fair. They had taken off their skin coverings, and were gowned in pale blue, and, as they danced about, their copper-colored hair streamed out behind their backs, glistening in the moonlight. He was delighted by their singing and amazed at their beauty.

At length he crept stealthily down the rock, and ran towards the skin coverings lying on the sand. He seized one and ran off with it. When the mermaids saw him they screamed and scattered in confusion, and snatching up their skin coverings, leaped into the sea and vanished from sight. One maid remained behind. This was the fair one round whom the others had been dancing.

One mermaid remained behind,
and she could not return to her sea home.

Her skin covering was gone, and so she could not return to her sea home.

Meanwhile the farmer ran to his house and hid the skin covering in a box, which he locked, placing the key in his pocket. He wondered what would happen next, and he had not long to wait. Someone came to his door and knocked softly. He stood listening in silence. Then he heard the knocking again, and opened the door. A Maid-of-the-Wave, clad in pale sea-blue garments, stood before him, the moonlight glistening on her wet copper hair. Tears stood in her soft blue eyes as she spoke sweetly, saying: "O man, have pity and give me back my skin covering so that I may return to my sea home."

She was so gentle and so beautiful that the farmer did not wish her to go away, so he answered: "What I have got I keep. Do not sorrow, O fair one. Remain here and be my bride."

The mermaid turned away and wandered along the shore, but the farmer did not leave his house. In the morning she returned again, and the farmer said to her: "Be my bride."

The mermaid consented, saying: "I cannot return to my fair sea home. I must live now among human beings, and I know no one except you alone. Be kind to me, but do not tell man or woman who I am or how I came here."

The farmer promised to keep her secret, and that day they were married. All the people of the township loved Maid-of-the-Wave, and rejoiced to have her among them. They thought she was a princess from a far country who had been carried away by the fairies.

For seven years the farmer and his wife lived happily together. They had three children, two boys and a girl, and Maid-of-the-Wave loved them dearly.

When the seventh year was drawing to a close the farmer set out on a journey to Big Town, having business to do there. His wife was lonely without him, and sat often on the shore singing songs to her baby girl and gazing over the sea.

One evening, as she wandered among the rocks, her eldest boy, whose name was Kenneth, came to her and

*His mother gasped with surprise and secret joy,
and asked softly, "Will you give me the key?"*

said: "I found a key which opened Father's box, and in
the box I saw a skin like the skin of a salmon, but
brighter and more beautiful, and very large."

His mother gasped with surprise and secret joy, and
asked softly: "Will you give me the key?"

Kenneth handed the key to her, and she hid it in her
pocket. Then she said: "It is getting late. The moon will
not rise till near midnight. Come home, little Kenneth,
and I shall make supper, and put you to bed, and sing
you to sleep."

As she spoke she began to sing a joyous song, and Kenneth was glad that his mother was no longer sad because his father was far from home. He grasped his mother's hand, and tripped lightly by her side as they went homeward together.

When the two boys had supper, and were slumbering in bed, the farmer's wife hushed her baby girl to sleep, and laid her in her cradle. Then she took the key from her pocket and opened the box. There she found her long-lost skin covering. She wished to return to her fair sea home, yet she did not want to leave her children. She sat by the fire for a time, wondering if she should put on the skin covering or place it in the box again. At length, however, she heard the sound of singing coming over the waves. Her sister mermaids were calling her home. After listening to their sweet songs, she knew she had to return to her home in the sea.

She kissed the two boys and wept over them. Then she knelt beside her little baby girl, who smiled in her sleep, and sang a song of farewell.

When she had sung this song she heard voices from the sea calling low and calling sweet, begging her to return to them.

The weeping mother kissed her boys and her baby girl once again. Then she put on her skin covering and, hastening down the beach, plunged into the sea. Before long, sounds of joy and laughter were heard far out amongst the waves, and they grew fainter and fainter until they were heard no more. The moon rose high and fair, and shone over the wide solitary ocean, and where the mermaids had gone no one could tell.

When the farmer returned next morning he found the children fast asleep. He wakened Kenneth, who told him about finding the key and opening the box.

"Where is the key now?" the farmer asked.

"I gave it to Mother," said the boy.

The farmer went towards the box. It was open, and the skin covering was gone. Then he knew what had happened, and sat down and wept because Maid-of-the-Wave had gone.

It is told that the lost mother often returned at night-time to gaze through the cottage windows on her children as they lay asleep. She left trout and salmon for them outside the door. When the boys found the fish they wondered greatly, and their father cried and said: "Your mother is far away, but she has not forgotten you."

"Will Mother return again?" the boys would ask.

"No, Mother will not return," their father would say. "She now dwells in the home of her people, to which you and I can never go."

When the boys grew up they became bold and daring seamen, and no harm ever came to them in storm or darkness, for their mother, Maid-of-the-Wave, followed their ship and protected it from all peril.

The Land of Green Mountains

RONALD BOOE HAD rebelled against his chief but was defeated in battle. Then all his followers deserted him, and he found that he would have to flee from his native land. It chanced that he had heard tell of the wonderful Land of Green Mountains near the world's end, in which there were great herds of wild animals, while fish could be caught in plenty round its shores and in its rivers. He made up his mind to go there and live happily and at ease. As he had no children, it was not difficult for him and his wife to depart in secret.

One fair morning they launched a boat and set sail. Ronald's heart was glad when he found himself far out on the wide blue sea. The broad grey sail swallowed the wind, and the creaking of the ropes was like sweet music in his ears. Ronald loved the shrill cry of the breeze that blew so steadily and tossed the sparkling brine-spray through the air in bright sunshine. The whisperings and mutterings of the waves that went past the boat seemed to repeat over and over again the old song of the sea:

> Sweet to me, Oh, sweet to me
> Is a life at sea, is a life at sea!

When the shore melted from sight, Ronald's wife felt very lonely and sad. "I wish," she said, "I could see the high brown hills of my own country."

Said Ronald: "There is no voyage so long that it will not come to an end. Speak not of brown hills, for we are voyaging to the wonderful Land of Green Mountains."

They sailed on and on for six days and six nights, and while the one slept the other sat at the helm. On the morning of the seventh day a storm arose. "Alas," the woman cried, "the boat will be dashed to pieces and we shall perish!"

Said Ronald: "Have no fear, Morag, daughter of Donald; am I not a skilled seaman? In storm and calm I am a king of the sea. My boat bounds over the waves like a spray-bright bird, and there is joy in my heart even in the midst of danger."

On the morning of the seventh day a storm arose.

The sky darkened, and the wind blew fiercer and louder, while the bounding waves gaped and bellowed like angry monsters seeking their prey. Crouching low, the woman moaned and wept with fear, until at length Ronald called to her, saying: "I see land ahead."

His wife rose up and gazed towards the horizon. With glad eyes she saw before her the wonderful Land of Green Mountains. Then she dried her tears and smiled.

It was not until late evening, however, that the boat drew near the shore. Ronald tried to steer towards a safe landing-place, but, while yet some distance from it, the boat struck a hidden rock and began to sink. Ronald grasped an oar with one hand and his wife with the other, and leaped into the raging sea. He was a strong swimmer, and, after a hard struggle, he managed to reach shallow water, and then wade ashore.

There was a cave near where he landed, and he carried his wife to it. Then he gathered dry sticks and withered grass and lit a fire by using flint and steel. Soon the flames were leaping high, and Ronald and his wife were able to dry their clothes. Then they lay down to sleep, and, although the sea roared all night long, they slept soundly.

Next morning Ronald found on the beach a keg of salt herring, a keg of meal, and a pot which had been washed ashore from the boat. His wife cooked the herring, and baked oatmeal cakes, and after the two had eaten them they felt quite happy.

A day or two went past, and then their supply of food ran short. Ronald had no weapons with which to hunt game, and no hooks with which to catch fish, so he said to his wife: "I will go inland and explore this strange Land of Green Mountains. Do not be anxious or afraid."

"You may lose your way," his wife said.

"There is no fear of that," Ronald answered. "I'll put marks on the trees as I go through forests, and set up stones on the plains I cross."

Early next morning Ronald set out on his journey. As he passed through the wood he chipped the bark off trees, and on the plain he set up stones. After leaving the wood, he saw a high green mountain, and walked towards it. "When I reach the top," he said to himself, "I shall get a better view of this strange land."

The sun was beginning to set when he found himself on the crest of the green mountain. He looked round about and could see many other green mountains, but there was no sign of human beings, and his heart grew very sad. Although he was very tired and very hungry, he did not despair, however. "I'll go down the other side of this green mountain," he said to himself, "and perhaps I shall have better luck."

He began to descend in the dusk, and before long he saw a light. It came from a little house among trees on the lower slope of the mountain, and he walked towards it. Darkness was coming on when he reached the house, and as the door was open he walked in.

To his surprise he found no one inside. A bright fire was burning, and near it stood a table and two chairs. The table was covered with a green cloth, and on it were two dishes of food.

"I am very hungry," said Ronald, "and must eat. I hope I shall not be blamed for helping myself."

He sat down and ate all the food that was on one of the plates. Then he felt happy and contented. Suddenly he heard the sound of footsteps, and, looking up, he saw an old grey-bearded man entering the house.

"Well, stranger," this man said, "who are you, and where have you come from?"

*"Well, stranger," an old grey-bearded man said,
"who are you, and where have you come from?"*

Ronald said: "My boat was wrecked on the shore. I have been wandering about all day searching for food, and found nothing until I came here. I hope you are not angry with me for eating without permission."

Said the old man: "You are welcome to my food. You can stay here tonight. I live all alone, and always keep enough food to give to any visitor who may come here as you have done."

Ronald thanked the old man for his kindness, and said: "I shall tell you all about myself in the hope that you may help me with good advice."

The old man sat down, and, as he ate his meal, Ronald told the story of his life. When he had finished the other asked: "Have you any children?"

"No," Ronald said, "I have no children."

"That is a pity," the old man sighed.

Next morning the old man wakened Ronald and said: "Breakfast is ready. It is time you were on your way back to the cave, for your wife is anxious and afraid."

When Ronald had eaten an excellent breakfast he said: "I wish I had food to carry to my wife."

Said the old man: "What will you give me for this green table-cloth? When you want food all you have to do is to shake it three times and lay it down. As soon as you lay it down you will get all the food you need."

Ronald was surprised to hear this. He looked at the green cloth, and, sighing, made answer: "Alas! I am very poor, having lost everything I possessed. I am not able to offer you anything for the green cloth."

Said the old man: "Will you promise to give me your eldest son for it?"

Having no son, Ronald promised quickly.

"Very well," the old man said, "come back here in seven years, and bring your son with you."

Ronald took the cloth, and said good-bye to the old man. He climbed the green mountain and went down the other side of it. Then he crossed the plain, past the stones he had set up, and walked through the wood, guiding himself by the marks he had made on the trees. He had no difficulty in finding his way. The sun was beginning to set as he reached the shore and hurried towards the cave, where he found his wife sitting beside the fire moaning and weeping. She feared her husband had been devoured by wild beasts.

"Here I am, Morag, daughter of Donald," he said as he entered the cave.

His wife rose to her feet and kissed him joyfully.

After he shook the green cloth three times, dishes of hot food appeared before their eyes.

"I have brought food for you," said Ronald.

As he spoke he shook the green cloth three times, and laid it on the floor of the cave beside the fire. As soon as he did that, two dishes of hot, steaming food appeared before their wondering eyes.

They sat down and ate the food. "Where did you find this wonderful green cloth?" asked Morag.

"It was given to me by an old grey-bearded man," Ronald told her. "Are we not in luck now? We shall never want for food as long as we live."

Several days went past. Then Ronald and his wife thought they would go inland and explore the country. They felt lonely, and wished to find out where the people who inhabited it had their dwellings.

For six days they travelled inland, and on the morning of the seventh day they reached a village. The people were kindly and hospitable and invited them to stay. Ronald thought he might as well do so, and next morning began to build a house. He got plenty of help from the villagers, and soon had a home of his own among his newly-found friends. Before the year was out a baby boy was born, and Ronald and Morag's hearts were filled with joy. They called the baby Ian.

Years went past, and Ian grew up to be a handsome boy with curly golden hair, sea-grey eyes, and red cheeks. Everyone in the village loved him, and he was very dear to his father and mother.

Ronald Booe remembered the promise he had made to the grey old man, but he never told Morag his wife about it until the seventh year was nearly at an end. Then one day he said: "Tomorrow I must go to the mountain house with Ian, because I promised the grey old man, when I was given the green cloth, to do so."

Morag cried: "Alas! alas!" and began to moan and weep. "It was foolish and wicked of you," she said, "to make such a promise."

Said Ronald: "What can I do? My heart bleeds to part with our boy, but I must go, and he must go with me."

Next morning he said good-bye to his wife, and she

kissed Ian and wept over him. Father and son then set out on their journey, and in time they reached the dwelling of the grey old man, who spoke, saying: "So you have come, as you said you would."

"Yes," Ronald answered sadly, "I have come."

"Do you find it hard to part with your boy?"

"Indeed, I do. My wife is heart-broken."

Said the grey old man: "You can take him home again if you promise me to come back when another seven years have gone past."

Ronald thanked the grey old man, and, having promised, he returned home with Ian. His wife welcomed him with smiling face and bright eyes, and kissed her child, saying, "If you had stayed away from me I should have died with sorrow."

Ian grew and grew, and when he was twelve years old he was nearly as tall as his father and nearly as strong. He had great skill as a hunter and as a fisherman, and could work in the fields like a man.

When the second term of seven years was drawing to a close his father grew sadder and sadder, and one day he said to his wife: "Tomorrow I must go to the mountain house with Ian."

"Alas! alas!" cried his wife; "I cannot live without him."

Said Ronald: "You cannot have your son beside you always. To every youth comes the day when he must leave his parents."

"Wait for a few years," pleaded Morag. "I have not long to live, and I want to have him beside me until I die."

Said Ronald: "It cannot be as you wish."

"Perhaps," his wife sighed, "the grey old man will send him back for another seven years."

Said Ronald: "He may, and he may not."

Next morning father and son set out on foot towards the mountain house, and when they reached it, the grey old man said: "So you have come as you promised. It is well. Do you find it hard to part with the lad?"

Said Ronald: "Indeed, I do. I find it harder now than I did seven years ago."

"Has the boy been well taught?" asked the old man.

Said Ronald: "He can fish, he can shoot, he can work in the fields. I have trained him myself."

"You have trained his body, but I will train his mind," the grey old man told Ronald. "Knowledge is better than strength. You will be proud of Ian some day."

The boy's father was stricken with sorrow when he found that the old man intended to keep Ian. He returned home alone. Morag wept bitterly when he entered the house, and all Ronald could say to comfort her was: "The grey old man promised that we should be proud of Ian some day."

Morag refused to be comforted, for she knew well that many years must pass before she would see her son again.

The grey old man was like a father to Ian. He spent six years in teaching the lad, and on the seventh he said: "Now you have passed your twentieth year. You are strong, and you are well educated. It is time you began to work for yourself. Before you go to look for a job, however, I shall take you on a long journey, so that you may meet friends who may help you in time of need. It is better to make friends than to make enemies."

Said Ian: "I am ready to do as you advise me."

"Well spoken!" the old man exclaimed. "You have learned to obey. He who learns how to obey will rise to command. Come with me to the mountain-top. Behind the door hangs a silver bridle. Take it with you."

Ian took the bridle and followed the old man. On the

mountain-top the old man said: "If you will shake the bridle over me I shall become a grey horse. You can then jump on my back, and we shall go forward quickly."

*Ian shook the bridle as he was asked to do,
and the man changed at once into a grey horse.*

Ian shook the bridle as he was asked to do. The man changed at once into a grey horse, and as soon as Ian mounted, the horse galloped away at a rapid pace. Over hill and over moor went the horse. Nor did it pause until seven hours went past. Then Ian heard the old man's voice, saying: "Dismount and shake the bridle over me."

Ian did as he was ordered, and the grey man at once returned to his own form again. He spoke, saying: "Go and gather red moss, and fill your water jug at the well below yonder red rock."

Ian gathered the moss, and filled his water jug, and returned to the old man, who said: "Go now to the cave which opens behind the waterfall. Inside it you will find a wounded giant. Dress his wounds with the red moss, and give him three drinks from your water jug."

Ian climbed down the side of the waterfall over slippery rocks, and when he entered the cave he saw the wounded giant. He put red moss on the giant's wounds, and bound it round with cords made of dried reeds. Then he gave the sufferer three drinks from his water jug. As soon as he did that, the giant sat up and cried out: "I am feeling better now. Before long I shall be well again."

"Remember me and be my friend," said Ian.

"Your friend I shall be," the giant answered.

Ian then returned to the old man, who asked him at once: "Have you done as I ordered you to do?"

"Yes," Ian answered.

"It is well," the old man told him. "Shake your bridle over me again, and then leap on my back, so that we may go forward quickly."

The old grey man in horse shape went galloping on and on, until a lonely shore was reached. Once more he called: "Shake the bridle over me," and when Ian had done so, the man appeared in his own form and said: "Go down the beach until you reach a flat brown stone. Behind that stone lies the King of Fish. Lift him up and put him into the sea, for this is a day of misfortune for him, and he is in need of help."

Ian ran down the long dreary sands until he reached the flat brown stone. He found the fish lying gasping and twitching and helpless. Lifting him up, Ian put him into the sea and, as he did so, cried out: "Remember me and be my friend."

The fish answered him, saying: "Your friend I shall be," and then vanished.

Ian returned to the old man and once again changed him into a horse. They went onward together, and before long reached a bronze castle on a lonely cliff overlooking the sea. It was now late evening. The old man said: "Enter the bronze castle, in which dwells a fair lady. You will see rooms full of silver and gold and flashing gems. Look at everything but touch nothing."

Ian went through the castle. He wondered to see so much treasure, but although it seemed to be unprotected, for he did not even see the fair lady, he never touched a single piece of gold or silver. When, however, he was leaving the castle, his eyes fell on a heap of goose feathers. He pulled out a single feather and put it in his pocket, but he did not tell the old man that he had done so.

He mounted the horse, and returned to the grey old man's hut in the gathering darkness, and there the two rested for the night.

Next morning the old man became a horse again, and carried Ian to the capital of the country—a large and beautiful city in the midst of which the king's castle stood on a high rock.

Outside the city wall Ian shook the bridle over the horse, and the old man stood before him and said: "Here we must part. You will go towards the castle, and ask for employment. The king is in need of a scribe. If he offers to employ you, accept his offer."

He pulled out a single feather and put it in his pocket.

Ian then said good-bye to the old man, who replied: "If ever you are in trouble, think of me and I shall come to you."

They parted at the western gate of the city, and Ian walked towards the castle. He told the guards that he was looking for employment, and after a time they took him before the chief scribe, who said: "I am in need of an assistant. Will you enter the king's service?"

Ian accepted the offer, and next morning began to work. He thought of the goose feather he had taken from the bronze castle, and made a pen of it. When he began to use it, he found that it wrote beautifully, and he was delighted at his own fine penmanship.

The head scribe was greatly surprised at the skill shown by the young man, and grew jealous of him. After a few days he asked Ian for the loan of his pen, and when he tried it he discovered that he could write just as well as Ian.

"This is a magic pen," he said to himself. He then went before the king and told him about it, and the king tried the pen also. "Bring this young scribe before me," he commanded.

Ian was called for, and when he stood before the king he was asked: "Where did you get this magic pen?"

Said Ian: "I found it in a bronze castle."

The king gazed at him in silence for a moment, and then spoke, saying: "There is a beautiful lady in that castle, and she cannot leave it. Bring her here, for I wish her for my bride."

Said Ian: "Alas! O king, I am not able to obey your command. I do not know where the castle is, for I was taken to it late in the evening, and returned home in the darkness."

"If you fail to do as I command," said the king, "you shall be put to death."

Ian went to his bedroom, and there wept tears of sorrow. He knew well that this trouble which had befallen him was due to his having disobeyed the old man, who had warned him not to touch anything he saw in the bronze castle. After a time he said aloud: "I wish the grey old man were here now." He heard a noise behind him, and, turning round, he saw the grey old man, who spoke, saying: "What is the matter, Ian?"

"Alas!" cried Ian, "I have done wrong." Then he told the old man how he had taken a goose feather from the bronze castle and made a quill of it, and that the king had discovered his secret, and ordered him to fetch the captive lady from the castle to be the king's bride.

"You should not have touched the feather," the old man said. "It is as wicked to steal a small thing as a great thing. Theft is dishonourable, even the theft of little things. I placed my trust in you, and you promised to obey me. Because you have failed in that trust and done this thing, you now find yourself in trouble."

"Alas!" Ian cried, "I know I have done wrong, and am sorry for it."

"Let this be a lesson to you," the old man said. "Because you are sorry for your wrongdoing, I shall help you once again. Let us go outside. I have the silver bridle with me. We shall visit the bronze castle once again."

Ian walked with the old man to a lonely place outside the city wall. There he shook the bridle, and his friend became a grey horse. He mounted and rode away swiftly towards the seaside. Then he shook the bridle again, and his friend appeared in human form and spoke to him, saying: "I have a magic rod. Take it and strike me with it. When you do so I shall become a ship. Enter the ship, and it will sail to the harbour below the bronze castle. Cast anchor there and wait until the lady looks out of a window and asks you where you have come from. Say: 'I have come from a distant land.' Then she will ask: 'What cargo do you have on board?' Say to her: 'I have a cargo of fine silk.' She will ask you to enter the castle with samples of the silk, but you will say: 'Would it not be better if you came on board and examined the rolls of silk?' She will answer: 'Very well,' and come on board your vessel. Take her down to the cabin, and spread out the rolls of silk you will find lying there."

Ian seized the magic rod and struck the grey old man,

Ian seized the magic rod,
and the old man became a large and noble ship.

who at once became a large and noble ship, afloat beside the rock. Ian got on board the ship, cast off from the rock, and set sail. It had a crew of little men clad in green, with red peaked caps on their heads. The skipper who steered the vessel had a long grey beard and sharp beady eyes. He never spoke a word, but gave orders to the crew by making signs.

The ship sailed swiftly towards the bronze castle on the lonely cliff. When the anchor was dropped in the little harbour Ian walked up and down the deck until an upper window in the castle opened, and the beautiful lady looked out and spoke to him, saying: "Where have you come from, my merry sailor man?"

"From a distant land," Ian answered.

"What cargo have you on board?"

"A cargo of fine silk."

"Come up into the castle and bring with you samples of your silk, and perhaps I may buy a few rolls from you."

Said Ian: "I have so many kinds of silk that I cannot carry samples to you. Would it not be better if you came on board and examined the cargo, O fair lady?"

"Very well," the lady answered. "I shall do as you suggest."

She came down from the castle and came on board the ship. Ian led her to the cabin, where he spread out before her the rolls of fine silk that he found there.

She examined them all carefully. Then hearing the splashing of waves against the sides of the ship, she ran up the cabin ladder to the deck, and discovered that the vessel was far away from the bronze castle.

"Alas!" she cried, "what is the meaning of this?"

Said Ian: "The king, my master, has ordered me to bring you before him. It is his wish that you should become his queen."

"It is your duty to obey your master, and I do not blame you," the lady said. "But I do not wish to be the king's bride. I should much rather have stayed yet a while in my bronze castle."

As she spoke, she took a bundle of keys from her waist-belt and flung it into the sea.

"There go my keys!" she told Ian. "No one else can now enter the bronze castle."

The ship sailed back to the place from which it had started, and drew up alongside the rock, and Ian and the lady went ashore. Then Ian waved the magic rod three times. When he did so the ship vanished, and the grey old man appeared by his side and spoke, saying: "Shake the silver bridle over me, so that I may become a horse. Mount me then, and take the lady with you."

Ian shook the bridle, and his friend became a grey horse. He mounted the horse, and the lady mounted behind him. They rode away very swiftly, and when night was coming on they reached the city. Ian shook the bridle again, and the old man appeared by his side, and they told each other good-bye. Ian led the lady to the castle and brought her to the king. His majesty thanked him for his service, and welcomed the lady. He called for maidservants to attend to her, and she was taken to her room.

Next morning the king had the lady brought before him, and said: "O fair one, be my bride."

Said the lady: "I shall not be your bride until my bronze castle is brought here and placed beside yours."

"No one can do that but Ian," the king said. Then he called to a servant, saying: "Bring Ian before me."

Ian had returned to his place in the room of the chief scribe, and was busy at his work when he was ordered to appear before his majesty.

He obeyed the summons, and the king said to him: "You must bring the bronze castle from the lonely cliff, and have it placed beside my castle."

"Alas!" Ian cried, "I cannot do that."

Said the king: "If you fail to carry out my command you shall be put to death."

Ian went to his room, and paced it up and down for a time, lamenting his fate. Then he cried out: "I wish the grey old man were here."

No sooner had he wished that wish than the grey old man appeared in the room and spoke to him, saying: "What is wrong now, Ian?"

Said Ian: "The king has set me an impossible task. He wants me to have the bronze castle carried here and placed beside his own castle."

"Come with me," the old man said.

Together they went outside the city wall. Ian shook the bridle over his friend, who at once became a grey horse. He mounted the horse, and rode away until he reached the waterfall behind which was the giant's cave. Then he shook the bridle again, and the old man appeared beside him and said: "Enter the cave and speak to the giant whose wounds you helped to heal. Tell him you are in need of his aid, and ask him to carry away the bronze castle and place it beside the castle of your king."

Ian went down the slippery rocks and entered the cave. He found the giant lying asleep on the floor, and walked towards him. As soon as he touched him the giant sat up and asked: "Who are you, and what brings you here, little fellow?"

Ian was at first too terrified to speak, for the giant scowled at him. At length he said: "I am he who dressed your wounds with red moss, and gave you three drinks of the healing water. I am now in need of your help."

Said the giant: "I remember you. I was in great pain, and you healed me. What do you wish me to do? Speak and I shall obey, even if you ask me to remove a mountain from its place and cast it into the sea."

Ian laughed aloud, and the giant laughed also, but the giant's laugh was terrible to hear, for it sounded like thunder.

Ian then told the giant that the king wished to have the bronze castle carried from the lonely cliff and placed beside his own castle on the rock in the midst of his capital.

Said the giant: "The work shall be done tonight. I shall call all my strong men together. Begone! or it may not go well with you."

Ian thanked the giant, and returned to the grey old man, who said: "We must hurry. There is no time to be lost."

As the grey horse, the old man travelled again swiftly until he reached the capital. Then he told Ian good-bye.

That night, as Ian lay in his bed, a great thunderstorm arose and raged furiously. He could not sleep, and lay trembling with fear, for it seemed as if the whole world would be set on fire by the flashes of lightning. When the thunder-storm was at its height, there came an earthquake. The rock beneath the castle trembled, and the castle swayed like a ship at sea. Ian was terrified, and he heard the shrieks of those who were even more afraid than he was. At length the storm died down, and he slept.

Next morning, when Ian looked through the window of his room, he saw the bronze castle beside the king's castle. Then he knew that the thunder-storm had been caused by the giants, and that the earth shook when they set down the castle upon the rock.

The rock beneath the castle trembled during the storm, and the castle swayed like a ship at sea.

The king was greatly pleased, and spoke to the fair lady, saying: "Your bronze castle has been brought here. Now you will be my queen."

Said the lady: "I cannot marry until I am given the bundle of keys I threw into the sea. The castle door cannot be opened without the keys."

"Ian shall find the keys," the king told her. Then he called for Ian and said to him: "You must find the bundle of keys which this fair lady threw into the sea."

"Alas!" Ian moaned, "you set me a task I cannot fulfil."

"If you do not bring the keys to me," said the king, "you shall be put to death."

Ian turned away and went to his room. He felt sure that his end was near at hand because it did not seem possible that the keys could be found. "I wish the old grey man were here," he cried out.

The old grey man appeared in the room and asked softly: "What does the king ask for now, Ian?"

Said Ian: "He has ordered me to find the bundle of keys which the fair lady threw into the sea."

"Come with me," the grey old man said; "we have a long journey before us."

Ian rode again on the grey horse until he reached the shore where he had found the King of Fish. He then shook the silver bridle and the old man appeared beside him. "Go out on the beach," he advised Ian, "and call for the King of Fish. When he comes, ask him to search for the keys and bring them to you."

Ian walked down the sands and called for the King of

The King of Fish gave him the keys and vanished at once.

Fish. Three times he called before the fish appeared. Then it rose and asked: "Who are you that you should call upon me?"—

Said Ian: "I am the one who found you lying behind the flat brown stone on a day of misfortune when you were in need of help. I lifted you up and put you into the sea, and you promised to remember me and be my friend."

"You speak truly," the fish said. "What is your wish? I am ready to grant it."

Said Ian: "Search for the keys which the fair lady of the bronze castle threw into the sea when I took her away in my ship. When you have found the keys, bring them to me."

The fish vanished and returned soon afterwards.

"Have you found the keys?" he asked.

"I have," answered the fish.

"Give them to me."

"I will give them if you promise one thing."

"What is that?"

"Promise that you will not call for me again."

"I promise," said Ian.

The fish then gave him the keys and vanished at once.

Ian was overjoyed. He ran up the beach towards the old man, who asked: "Have you got the keys?"

"Oh, yes!"

"It is well. Shake the bridle over me and mount."

Ian did so, and rode back to the capital on the back of the grey horse. Having said good-bye to his friend, he hurried before the king and handed the keys of the bronze castle to him.

"It is good for you that you found the keys," the king said. "Had you come back without them you would have been put to death."

Ian bowed and turned away, hoping that his troubles were at an end.

The king sent for the lady of the castle and said: "Here are the keys of the bronze castle which my servant found for me."

"He is a brave and noble lad," the lady cried out.

"Now you will marry me," said the king.

"I cannot promise to marry you, O king, until I get a jug of water from the Healing Well."

Said the king: "I shall order Ian to bring the water without delay."

He sent for Ian, and spoke to him harshly, saying: "Bring here without delay a jug of water from the Healing Well."

"Where is that well, O king?" asked Ian.

"I know not," was the answer. "But this I know: if you do not bring the water you will be put to death."

Ian went to his room and wished for the grey old man, who appeared at once and asked: "What's the matter now, my poor lad?"

"Alas!" Ian exclaimed, "the king has asked for a jug of water from the Healing Well, but he does not know where it is."

"We had better hurry and search for it."

Away went Ian again on the back of the grey horse. All day long he rode over hill and dale, through forests and across bogs, over rivers and through lakes, until at length a lonely valley was reached.

"Shake the bridle," called the horse.

Ian shook it, and the old man stood beside him and said: "Strike me with the magic wand and I shall fall down dead."

"I cannot do that," Ian answered at once.

"You must do it. When I am dead three ravens will fly here. Speak to them, saying: 'I shall kill you with my wand unless you take me to the Healing Well.' They will then show you where it is. When you find it, fill two jugs and bring them to this spot. Sprinkle a few drops of the water in my mouth, in my eyes, and in my ears. When you do so, I shall come to life again."

Ian struck the old man with the magic wand and he fell down dead. He lay so still that the young man's heart was filled with sorrow, and he began to weep. "Would that the ravens were here!" he cried out, as he looked round about. To his amazement he saw no sign of the ravens coming.

For over an hour he sat there beside his dead friend, fearing that he would never be able to bring him back to life again.

But at length the ravens came, and Ian stood up and called out: "I shall kill you with my magic wand if you do not do as I tell you."

"What is your wish?" the ravens asked him in turn.

Said Ian: "Lead me to the Healing Well."

The ravens flew round about above him three times, and then cried out, one after the other: "Follow, follow me."

Ian followed them, and was led to a dark and lonely ravine in which there was a deep cave. The ravens entered the cave, and Ian followed them. Inside he heard the dripping of water, but he saw nothing, for the place was very dark.

Said one of the ravens: "Dip your jugs in the pool beside which you stand."

Ian did so, and he lifted them up full of water. Joyfully he hastened out of the cave, and returned to the spot where he had left the old man. He sprinkled water drops in his eyes, in his ears, and in his mouth. When he had done so the old man rose up and said: "Shake the bridle over me."

Ian was soon again on the back of the grey horse. When he returned to the castle it was almost midnight. He carried the jugs to his room, and in the morning gave one of them to the king.

The king called for the fair lady, and he handed her the jug of water and said: "Now you will marry me."

Said the lady: "I cannot marry you until you have fought a duel with Ian. He has done what you cannot do, and is now more powerful than you are."

"You speak truly," the king answered. "This duel must be fought at once."

He called a court attendant and told him to hurry to Ian and tell him to prepare for the duel.

Ian was amazed to hear this command, and when he was alone he wished for the grey old man, who appeared and asked at once: "What is wrong now, Ian?"

Ian told him that the king desired to fight a duel.

Said the grey old man: "Wash all your body with the water from the Healing Well. No weapon can wound you when you have done that. I have brought a sword for you."

He handed a small sword to Ian and then vanished.

Ian washed himself with the water from the Healing Well, and then went forth to fight the duel with the king.

Said the fair lady: "He who wins the duel will marry me, and reign over the Land of Green Mountains. Is that not so, O king?"

The king was very vain, and was certain that she expected him to win the duel. He despised Ian with his small sword, and raised his own to strike him. But although he struck Ian three times he could not wound him. Then Ian struck once and the king fell dead.

"Hail to the new king!" called the lady of the bronze castle.

All the people called out: "Hail to the king!"

The king despised Ian with his small sword,
and raised his own to strike him.

So Ian was crowned king, and he married the fair lady. His friend, the grey old man, came to the wedding, bringing Ian's father and mother with him.

"Did I not promise you that you would be proud of Ian some day?" said the grey old man to Ronald Booe and Morag, daughter of Donald.

Before they could answer, Ian came forward. He embraced and kissed his mother, and shook his father's right hand, and then said: "You shall stay here with me for the rest of your days."

Ian was a wise and good king, and he and his queen were greatly beloved by their people. Indeed, there was never such a king in the Land of Green Mountains as Ian, son of Ronald Booe and of Morag, daughter of Donald.

THE END